# ESCAPE

A BILLIONAIRE ISLAND NOVELLA

HELEN HARDT

*To all the Wolfes of Manhattan fans... Welcome to Billionaire Island!*

ALSO BY HELEN HARDT

Gems of Wolfe Island

*Moonstone*

*Raven*

Billionaire Island

*Escape*

Follow Me Series:

*Follow Me Darkly*

*Follow Me Under*

*Follow Me Always*

*Steel Brothers Saga*:

Trilogy One—Talon and Jade

*Craving*

*Obsession*

*Possession*

Trilogy Two—Jonah and Melanie

*Melt*

*Burn*

*Surrender*

Trilogy Three—Ryan and Ruby

*Shattered*

*Twisted*

*Unraveled*

Trilogy Four—Bryce and Marjorie

## PRAISE FOR HELEN HARDT

### WOLFES OF MANHATTAN

"It's hot, it's intense, and the plot starts off thick and had me completely spellbound from page one."

**~The Sassy Nerd Blog**

"Helen Hardt...is a master at her craft."

**~K. Ogburn, Amazon**

"Move over Steel brothers... Rock is *everything!*"

**~Barbara Conklin-Jaros, Amazon**

"Helen has done it again. She winds you up and weaves a web of intrigue."

**~Vicki Smith, Amazon**

### FOLLOW ME SERIES

“Hardt spins erotic gold...”

**~*Publishers Weekly***

“22 Best Erotic Novels to Read”

**~*Marie Claire* Magazine**

“Intensely erotic and wildly emotional...”

**~*New York Times* bestselling author Lisa Renee Jones**

“With an edgy, enigmatic hero and loads of sexual tension, Helen Hardt's fast-paced Follow Me Darkly had me turning pages late into the night!”

**~*New York Times* bestselling author J. Kenner**

“Christian, Gideon, and now...Braden Black.”

**~Books, Wine, and Besties**

“A tour de force where the reader will be pulled in as if they're being seduced by Braden Black, taken for a wild ride, and left wanting more.”

**~*USA Today* Bestselling Author Julie Morgan**

“Hot. Sexy. Intriguing. Page-Turner. Helen Hardt checks all the boxes with *Follow Me Darkly!*”

**~International Bestselling Author Victoria Blue**

**STEEL BROTHERS SAGA**

"*Craving* is the jaw-dropping book you *need* to read!"

**~*New York Times* bestselling author Lisa Renee Jones**

"Completely raw and addictive."

**~#1 *New York Times* bestselling author Meredith Wild**

"Talon has hit my top five list...up there next to Jamie Fraser and Gideon Cross."

**~*USA Today* bestselling author Angel Payne**

"Talon and Jade's instant chemistry heats up the pages..."

**~RT Book Reviews**

"Sorry Christian and Gideon, there's a new heartthrob for you to contend with. Meet Talon. Talon Steel."

**~Booktopia**

"Such a beautiful torment—the waiting, the anticipation, the relief that only comes briefly before more questions arise, and the wait begins again... Check. Mate. Ms. Hardt..."

**~Bare Naked Words**

"Made my heart stop in my chest. Helen has given us such a heartbreakingly beautiful series."

**~Tina, Bookalicious Babes**

**BLOOD BOND SAGA**

“An enthralling and rousing vampire tale that will leave readers waiting for the sequel.”

**~Kirkus Reviews**

"Dangerous and sexy. A new favorite!"

**~*New York Times* bestselling author Alyssa Day**

“A dark, intoxicating tale.”

**~Library Journal**

“Helen dives into the paranormal world of vampires and makes it her own.”

**~Tina, Bookalicious Babes**

“Throw out everything you know about vampires—except for that blood thirst we all love and lust after in these stunning heroes—and expect to be swept up in a sensual story that twists and turns in so many wonderfully jaw-dropping ways.”

**~Angel Payne, *USA Today* bestselling author**

## 1

## EMILY

I stop looking over my shoulder on the fourth day.

I don't notice this until the evening, when I sit down by myself at the bar. I've been at the Wolfe Island—nicknamed Billionaire Island—Art Colony less than a week, but until today, I've been watching my back.

When you're hiding from the devil himself, you don't let your guard down.

A second after sitting down on the wooden stool at the beachfront bar, I look behind me.

That's when I realize it's the first time I've done it today.

Whether that's good or bad, I can't say. I shouldn't be getting too comfortable.

"What'll it be, pretty girl?"

I shift my gaze toward the bartender's deep voice—

And nearly drop my jaw onto the counter. His eyes

are such a gorgeous mixture of emerald and cognac. Most would simply call them hazel. I see a swirl of Prussian green and olive green with hints of Renaissance gold.

Believe it or not, those amazing eyes pale in comparison to the rest of him.

I smile shyly. I've kept to myself since I arrived on the island, spending most of my time painting the scenes outside my hut. This is the first time I've ventured to the beach.

"You going to answer me?" Hunky bartender raises his dark brown eyebrows.

"Yeah. Sorry." My cheeks burn. "Just some water, I guess."

"You guess? You can do better than that, pretty girl."

*Pretty girl.* The second time he's called me that in the span of two minutes. I don't feel pretty. On the outside, I suppose I'm okay. On the inside, a disaster.

"Cat still got your tongue?" He smiles a lazy smile that makes him even better looking. "Trust me?"

I part my lips and lick them. Trust him? I trust no one. *No one.* He has no idea what kind of can of worms he's opened.

"I'll take that as a yes." He reaches under the bar and pulls out a martini glass.

I hate martinis, but still I say nothing.

"Try my specialty. Virgin?"

My jaw drops. "Of course not!"

He laughs. "I mean do you want the virgin version of my specialty?"

"Oh." God, my cheeks can't get any hotter. I can only imagine what they look like in the light of the setting sun. "That's what I meant. I don't want the virgin one."

"Got it." He smiles.

Yeah, he doesn't buy it, but I give him credit for letting me try to weasel out of my embarrassment.

He turns toward the back of the bar and pulls three different bottles from the myriad options.

Three bottles? Maybe I should have gone with the virgin.

He fills a stainless steel shaker with crushed ice and adds a stream of the golden, the yellow, and the hot pink. I eye the bottle closest to me—the pink one. Crème de Noyaux. Never heard of it.

Next he adds what appears to be orange juice and then pineapple. A Mai Tai maybe? No, he said it was his specialty. Surely he didn't invent the Mai Tai. Or maybe he invented this particular version.

He adjusts the lid and shakes several times. Once he's done, he slides a slice of lime around the rim of the martini glass, dips it in sugar, and then strains the contents of the shaker into the glass.

I notice the color first. It's a lovely pinkish-orange, the shade of last night's sunset that I tried to capture on canvas but couldn't.

He pushes the drink toward me and sets a cocktail napkin next to it. "Tell me what you think."

Good enough. I inhale and pick the martini glass up by its stem. I sniff. Nice fragrance. Orangey and almondy. Very tropical.

"Well?" he says. "Are you waiting for a little umbrella?"

I can't help myself. I laugh. I laugh like I haven't in a long time, and it feels good. Really good.

"You got one?" I ask.

"Your wish is my command." He reaches under the counter and then pops a tiny pink umbrella into my drink.

If I had my phone, I'd shoot a pic and post this on Instagram.

I don't have my phone, though, and I deleted all my social media accounts.

In fact, the only person who has a clue where I am is my brother, Buck, and he's sworn to secrecy. He helped me get the invitation to the colony when I needed to leave town in a hurry. The person I'm running from can't touch Buck.

No one can.

"I'm out of dry ice. Otherwise, I'd put a tiny chunk in the drink and fog would swirl out of it."

The bartender's deep voice jolts me out of my thoughts. Just as well. I hate thinking about what brought me here. I prefer to think about why anyone else comes here—to learn, to grow, to create.

And probably to meet a gorgeous bartender with a bronze tan, broad shoulders, dark hair that falls below his ears, and eyes that seem to pierce a woman's soul. Even in the bright blue island shirt with palm trees and flamingos—this guy pulls it off as if it's this season's Armani.

"I ordered a bunch for Halloween next month," he continues. "I'm working on some great new concoctions." He eyes the drink I still haven't tasted. "What are you waiting for, pretty girl?"

I grab the stem of the glass once more and bring the drink to my lips.

Flavor explodes across my tongue. Pineapple, orange, banana, almond. And rum. A *lot* of rum. I swallow.

"Well…?" he says.

"It's delicious." I swallow again, this time against the sharpness of the alcohol.

He smiles. "Too much?"

I return his smile this time. "Nope. Just enough."

# 2

# SCOTTY

"What's your name, pretty girl?"

I admit it. I call them all "pretty girl." This one, though, gives new meaning to the phrase. "Pretty girl" isn't nearly descriptive enough for her long dark hair, deep brown eyes, rosy cheeks, and dark pink lips. And that body...

She's tall and slim with breasts that are spilling out of her halter top.

"Emily. What's yours?"

"Keanu."

She smiles. "No shit?"

"My mom's a big fan. Plus, I'm half Hawaiian. Everyone around here calls me Scotty."

"Why?"

"That's my last name. Scott. Not Reeves."

"Ah. Got it."

"What's your last name, pretty Emily?"

She falters a moment. Then, "Smith."

Smith. Nice try. I'm more likely to believe it's Hornswoggle than Smith, especially after she stumbled.

"Okay, Emily Smith. Nice to meet you."

She clears her throat softly. "You too."

"What brings you here? Are you an artist?"

"I'm trying to be."

"This is the place for you, then. Roy and Charlie Wolfe are great. Both really talented too."

She nods. "I haven't met them yet. I just got here a few days ago."

"A few days ago? And I'm just now seeing you? Where've you been?"

"In my room, mostly."

"Emily, you've got this gorgeous island at your disposal and you've been in your room?"

"Not the whole time," she says. "But the view from my lanai is breathtaking. I've been painting it every day."

"Look around you, pretty girl. This whole *place* is breathtaking. I consider myself lucky every day that I landed this gig."

She takes another sip of the drink and winces. Yeah, it *is* pretty strong, but I've never had anyone not love it.

"What's this called?" she asks.

"It doesn't really have a name. It's just my special drink."

"Seriously? It doesn't have a name?"

"No. Why should it?"

"Because it's delicious. It should be in that book. What's it called? *The Boston Bartender*?"

"You mean *Mr. Boston Official Bartender's Guide*."

"Yeah. That one."

I laugh. "That'll be the day."

"Why not? It's wonderful."

"I'm sure it's been done before."

"I've never heard of anything called Keanu Scotty Scott's special drink."

She's got me there. "Tell you what," I say. "*You* can name the drink."

She swallows her latest sip. "Me?"

"Sure. Why not? You're the one who thinks it's supposed to have a name."

"I'll have to think on it." She takes another sip and then sets the drink down on the coaster I provided. "What's Crème de Noyaux?"

"It's a liqueur made from apricot kernels or peach and cherry pits. Which is weird, because it tastes like almonds."

"What makes it pink?"

"It's a chemical reaction from the acid in the pits when the sugars ferment into alcohol."

"Really?" She widens her eyes. "Interesting."

I smile. I've given that bogus explanation to many a female since I created the drink during my first bartending gig in Honolulu, and every single one of them has bought it. For some reason, women always want to know why the liqueur is pink.

Take that back. A chemical engineer—who was hot as hell, by the way—called me out. Other than her, though, everyone has bought it—and I still got her between the sheets.

For some reason, though, lying to Emily unnerves me. I have no idea why. Certainly not her looks. I've put one over on my share of beautiful women.

"I'm kidding," I say. "It's artificially colored."

She looks. "I suppose I might know that if I were more worldly."

"Trust me. A lot of really intelligent women have fallen for it. Doesn't mean you're not worldly."

"I'm not," she says. "At least, I don't want to be."

"Oh? What do you want to be, then?"

She sighs. "Right now? I just want to be invisible."

I shake my head and grin. "You're way too beautiful to ever be invisible."

Her cheeks redden. So do the tops of her breasts.

Damn.

"Thank you," she says finally.

"No thanks needed. You want another?" I point to her nearly empty cocktail glass.

She shakes her head. "I should probably quit while I'm ahead. I haven't eaten anything since breakfast."

"Oh? I'm just about off the clock. Want to grab dinner with me?"

The words tumbled out of my mouth before I could

stop them. I've been working here for a couple months —since the colony opened. It's a dream gig, and getting involved with the colonists is probably not the best way to keep it. What am I thinking?

Easy answer. I'm thinking I might die a little if she says no.

"I should get back," she says.

"Oh. Sure. I understand."

"It's just..."

"Hey, you don't owe me any explanation, p— Emily."

She smiles then, and it's like a holiday carol. Bright and beautiful and joyous. God, what's the matter with me?

"You know what, Keanu?"

"Scotty."

"Okay." Her smile brightens further. "Scotty. I think I'd like to get some dinner. When are you off?"

I glance at my phone that's sitting on the end of the bar. "Just about...now." I was off ten minutes ago, actually, but Emily took precedence. I shove the phone in my pocket and pull my signature move.

I jump over the bar and land next to her.

"Goofball," Lyle, who's taking the next shift, says under his breath.

I ignore him. He's my pal and makes a mean drink, but he can fuck off at the moment.

I hold out my arm, and Emily pauses a second before she links her own through it.

Yeah, this beautiful woman is definitely hiding something. Maybe I'll get her to open up.

Or at least open her legs.

I wouldn't mind tapping what's between them.

Wouldn't mind that at all.

## 3

## EMILY

"What do you feel like tonight?" Scotty asks me.

"I have no idea."

"It's mostly island food, but it you want something American, we can go to the burger bar."

Truth be told, I haven't been to any of the restaurants here at the colony. I've either ordered room service or had food delivered beachside when I left the room to attend a class. Now, I'm a little freaked.

"A burger's fine."

"A burger it is, then." We step up to the burger bar. It's not a bar so much as a sit-down place with tables. All the eateries here at the colony are outdoor, covered in thatch roofing, of course, in case of rain, which sometimes occurs in the afternoons. Still, it's always so warm that having no walls doesn't matter.

A scantily clad hostess takes us to a table for two. "Your server will be with you in a minute."

"What's your pleasure?" Scotty picks up the menu on the side of the table.

"Just a basic burger."

"Cheese?"

"No. I'm one of those weird people who doesn't like cheese on a burger." True story. It takes away from the flavor of the meat, in my opinion.

"Heathen!" He smiles.

"Hey, Scotty." A nice-looking man in an island print shirt—this one yellow with tropical flowers, and even louder than Scotty's—and surf shorts struts up. "Who's your friend?"

"Hey, Nemo. This is Emily."

"You an artist?" Nemo asks.

I nod. "I try to be."

"Welcome. When did you arrive?"

"Four days ago."

"Really? Most people from the states can't wait to try the burgers here."

I have no idea what to say, so I say nothing.

"I'll have the usual," Scotty says, nodding to me.

"What's the usual?" I ask.

Nemo laughs. "You don't want to know!"

I raise my eyebrows at Scotty.

"The staff makes fun of me. It's a double, medium rare, with horseradish cheddar, green chili sauce, and a fried egg."

"Ugh." I twist my lips into a grimace.

"Don't knock it till you've tried it," Scotty laughs.

"I don't do eggs," I tell him. "They're gross."

"That's it." Scotty shakes his head with another smile. "It's over between us."

It's a joke, I know, but still warmth creeps to my cheeks. I didn't come here to have a fling. I came here to...

God. So don't want to think about that at the moment.

"I'll have a single, medium, with lettuce, tomato, and pickle."

"One basic American, sans cheese." Nemo scribbles on his pad.

"That's me," I say. "Just a basic American."

"Pretty girl"—Scotty smiles—"there's nothing basic about you that I can see."

Basic. Such an innocuous word. What I wouldn't give to actually be a basic American at the moment. Just another girl no one notices.

Invisible.

Invisibility has its perks.

"So here we are," Scotty says, after Nemo leaves, "one Scotty and one basic American."

"Your burger is called the Scotty?"

"Sure is. No one else orders it."

"Shocking." I take a drink of the water Nemo left for us.

He laughs.

"So the burger you invented has a name, but your special drink doesn't?"

"Yup."

"That makes no sense at all."

"Just never found the right name," he says, "and now I know why. You were meant to name it, pretty girl."

I swallow another drink of water.

Feelings bubble inside me. Feelings I don't want to have. I came here to escape. To be invisible. The last thing I need is to start down this road.

Scotty's probably just being nice. He's a bartender on a tropical island, for God's sake. He probably beds someone new each week. Each day, even.

I clear my throat. "How long have you been tending bar?"

"Here? Just since the colony opened a few months ago. Before that I was at a resort on Fiji."

"And you're from Honolulu?"

He nods. "Born and raised. My mom's a native, and my dad's a fighter pilot from LA."

LA. I don't mean to react, but my facial muscles tighten.

"Where are you from, pretty girl?"

"Portland," I lie. I don't want anyone to know I'm from LA. I've escaped LA, at least for now.

"Portland, Oregon?"

"You know another one?"

He laughs. "No."

"Yes. Portland, Oregon."

"Tell me about the Pacific Northwest. I've only been to California. And to Florida once when I was a kid."

"You didn't travel much outside the islands?"

He shakes his head. "Nope. I'm an island boy through and through. We traveled to Cali once in a blue moon to see my dad's folks, but mostly they came to us. People love to visit Hawaii, for some reason."

"I can't imagine why." Especially if all the men look like him.

"Big tourist trap if you ask me. Once you do Diamond Head and the Pearl Harbor thing, there's not much to do except lounge on the beach."

"I think that's probably the point," I say.

"I suppose. When you grow up there, it's not nearly as exciting."

"Really? If that's the case, why are you working on another beach?"

He laughs. Really laughs this time, like I've just said something hilarious during a standup routine.

"You got me, pretty girl. I'm a beach bum through and through."

"So you can't fault others for wanting just a taste of that life, then."

"I don't. It's just... I don't know. Every once in a while I wonder if there's more out there for me, you know?"

"Why bartending?" I ask.

"Why not?"

I shake my head and swallow another drink of water. "Are you ever serious about anything?"

"Sure I am. I seriously think you're the most beautiful woman I've seen since I got here. And this is a tropical island, pretty girl. I may have only been here for a few months, but gorgeous women are at a premium."

"At an art colony?"

"Sure. Some of the artists. And the women who work here. I swear Roy Wolfe only hired good-looking people."

"I think you just gave yourself a huge compliment," I can't help saying.

"I'm talking about the female population," he says, "but hey, if the shoe fits."

I laugh. Truly laugh.

And I realize Keanu Scotty Scott is the first person who's made me do that in...how long?

A long time.

A long, long time.

## 4

## SCOTTY

Nemo drops off our order.

"Dig in," I say to Em.

Already she's Em to me. Em or pretty girl. Emily is too stuffed-shirt a name for this dark-haired beauty. She's Em, the goddess of art. Is there even a goddess of art? Probably somewhere in Greek or Roman mythology, but I don't have a clue.

Only one goddess in front of me. Em.

She picks up her burger carefully and takes a bite. "Oh!" Grease runs down her chin.

"Forgot to mention. These are the juiciest burgers ever."

She wipes her mouth with her napkin. "I see."

"Burgers are an American thing," I say, "but I swear Diego does them better than anyone in the states. Not that I'd know, since I haven't been there in forever."

"Diego?"

"He's the chef here."

"Of all the food?"

"Just this place. Burgers are his specialty. He's a master."

"I'll say." She swallows and wipes her lips again. "This is delicious."

I take a bite of my Scotty classic. To make Em feel better, I let the juice and egg yolk drip from my lips a little before I clear it away with my napkin. Honestly, the dripping's the best part. Seems to make me enjoy the food even more.

"Tell mc your life story," I say.

She flinches a little. Only a little, but I notice. I notice everything about her. The curve of her jawline. The one freckle on her upper lip. The way her left eye squints slightly when she smiles.

"Not much to tell," she finally replies.

"How did you end up here?"

"I'm an artist. This is what I do."

"I get that, but most people pay a lot to be here. You must be a successful artist."

She flinches just a little once more. Then, "I do okay."

"Yeah?"

"But I'm not paying to be here," she says. "A fellowship opened up, and I got it."

"Good for you! You must be uber talented, then."

She takes another bite of her burger and chews. And chews. The meat and bun must be masticated into mash by the time she swallows. "Like I said, I do okay."

I swallow a drink of my water. "What are you hiding, pretty girl?"

"Nothing," she says way too quickly, dropping her gaze.

Nothing my ass. But I won't push it. Not my business. I don't have to know her life story to get her in the sack.

Except that I *want* to know her life story. Already I'm feeling a connection that's new to me. New...and a little frightening. But I've never been one to back down in the face of fear.

"Tell me about your work," I say.

"Modern, mostly. Oils. But since I've been here, I've been concentrating on the beauty of my surroundings. The colors are so vivid and bright. I swear, sunrises and sunsets don't look this way in El— Portland."

"Not with all that smog," I agree, deciding consciously not to comment on her stumble.

"I've started three different projects just from the view of my lanai," she continues. "I love mixing color, and these are some new shades I've never worked with before. Plus all the flora. Tropical flowers are something else. And everything's so green! Even the palm trees are greener than the ones at home."

"Are they?"

"They seem to be. To me, at least."

Her eyes light up when she speaks of color. Not surprising, given she's an artist. But I can't help but notice the light in those gorgeous browns is short-lived.

Yup, definitely hiding something.

"You want to take a walk on the beach after dinner?" I ask.

"Don't you have to go back to the bar?"

"Nope. I work days. Nine to four with a half hour for lunch."

"People drink that early?"

"Some do. We also have an awesome juice bar. You should come by in the morning and I'll make you one of my special blends."

She smiles. "You have a specialty for just about everything, huh?"

"Not going to lie. I do." I polish off the rest of my burger.

Em's sits half-eaten on her plate.

"Not hungry?" I ask.

"I am, and it's delicious. It's just so big."

"I guess I should have warned you. The single is a half-pound of meat."

Her eyes go wide. "You just ate a pound of beef!"

"Nah. The doubles are made with third-pound burgers. Though I could easily put away a pound."

She rakes her gaze over me. "How do you eat like that and stay in such great shape?"

I waggle my eyebrows. "Like what you see?"

She blushes. Adorably. Man, she's fucking hot.

"I'd say yes," she says, "but I'm pretty sure you turn

on the charm with every woman who sidles up to your bar."

She's not wrong. "Maybe. They don't all get a dinner invitation, though."

"Dinner's free," she says. "The colony is all inclusive."

"So it is. But, pretty girl, I'd gladly take you out and pay for the finest dinner on the island. We'd have to go across to the resort, though, and it doesn't open for another month."

She blushes even redder. "I don't know what you're after, Scotty, but I'm pretty sure I don't have it."

"Who says I'm after anything?"

"I know the type. I'm from LA, remember? You're a typical beach bum who beds a new woman every week. I'm not gunning to become a notch on your bedpost."

Yeah. I've heard those words before. Many times. And almost every time, I've gotten the woman who uttered them into my bed despite her protestations. But that's not what concerns me at the moment. This wasn't a mere stumble. I raise an eyebrow. "LA? Not Portland?"

Her cheeks turn crimson and she drops her gaze to her unfinished burger.

"Why'd you lie, Em?"

She twists her lips and then finally lifts her head to meet my gaze. "I'm sorry. I..."

"It's okay," I say. "You don't have to explain."

"No. I do, actually. I got too comfortable too quickly.

I let my guard down. I shouldn't even be here talking to you." She stands.

I rise as well. "Sit, Em. Please. It's okay. I'm not angry at you for lying. And if you can't let your guard down here, on a beautiful island, I don't know where you can."

"I can't," she says. "Not here. Not anywhere."

She's frightened. The fear rolls off her in waves.

I could walk away. Easy. Walk away from whatever she's carrying around.

Except I don't want to.

Is it the fact that she's hot? No. She's far from the only hot woman available at the colony. No, it runs deeper. She's hiding something, and I find myself caring about it.

About her.

## 5

## EMILY

"About that walk on the beach?" Scotty says.

I shouldn't have lied to him, but I was trying to maintain distance. That didn't work out so well. Already Scotty has me feeling too comfortable. Giddy, even. Like I've had a couple drinks, except it's been over an hour since my Scotty special at the bar.

Maybe Lucifer won't find me here. Maybe I truly am safe.

I shudder without meaning to.

Just his name—Lucifer. He's not actually the devil, of course, but Lucifer *is* his real name. Lucifer Charles Ashton III. Yes, he's the third in his line to actually bear the first name Lucifer.

And boy, has he lived up to the name.

He's known in the LA underground as Lucifer Black. Ironically, he's blond, but despite his coloring, he's full of darkness.

I was seduced by that darkness. By his power. By his seductive male beauty and his lavish gifts.

I let myself get comfortable, painting in my room. When I went to the bar earlier and met Scotty, I realized I hadn't looked over my shoulder at all today.

Until now.

A walk on the beach...

The gorgeous white sand beach beckoned from the moment I arrived. Artists with easels sat on their portable stools painting all day and even continued after the sun went down.

I've ventured to the beach exactly twice for classes, ordering a quick sandwich and throwing a few strokes on canvas, until that niggling on the back of my neck got unbearable, and I left. I've painted mostly from my lanai. I haven't taken advantage of this beautiful place, but I have my reasons.

One reason, actually.

A reason that wants me back in LA. Either back in LA, at his side...

Or dead.

Damn! Where is that easy relaxation I felt only hours ago sitting at the bar with Scotty?

"You going to answer me?" he finally says.

I inhale. The beach. I'm here, at the colony. Who wouldn't want to walk on the beach? I could feign illness, but he just watched me eat. Besides, I like Scotty. I don't want to tell him a little white lie, especially after my first one blew up in my face.

I don't want to tell him *any* lies, which is why I shouldn't talk to him at all.

"I'm kind of tired," I say. A little white lie after all. So much for that plan.

"It's seven o'clock."

"Yeah, but I'm still on LA time. We're five hours behind here. Plus, jet lag and all."

"Didn't you get here three days ago? Or was it four?"

I let out a huff. "For God's sake, Scotty. I'm not interested. Okay?" Yeah, the lies are just rolling out of my mouth now.

"I call bullshit," he says.

"Call it whatever you want. I didn't come here to hook up. I came here to—"

"To hide," he finishes for me.

"To *paint*. I came here to paint."

"Then why'd you show up at the beach bar?" he asks.

I don't have an answer. At least not one that makes sense.

"Just felt like a drink." I shrug.

"And then you accepted my invitation to dinner."

"A girl's got to eat."

"I see." He sighs. "Okay, I get it."

I nod. "Thanks for dinner. And the drink." Though he didn't pay for either. The art colony is all-inclusive.

"No sweat off my back."

"Yeah. I suppose not. So I'll see you around?"

"I'm sure you will. I work here."

I've upset him. And the truth is, I really do want to go on a walk with him. I like this guy. I wasn't sure I ever wanted to like a guy again, but Scotty wormed his way under my skin in record time.

And boy, is he good-looking. The best-looking guy I've seen in a while, and I'm used to LA beach boys. They don't come hotter than that.

Except here on Billionaire Island, apparently.

"You know what?" I say. "Let's live in the moment."

"Baby, that's what I always do."

"Let's take that walk. It's just a walk, right?"

"It's whatever you want it to be."

I cock my head. "You'll be okay if it's just a walk?"

"Em, listen to me. You're beautiful. If I tell you I'm not attracted to you, you won't believe me. Would I love to watch the sunrise with you? Hell, yeah. I'm human. But I'm also not a damned rapist. Sometimes a cigar is just a cigar. Sometimes a walk is just a walk."

Crap. Now I've pissed him off.

"Freud," I say.

"What about him?"

"Your cigar comment. It's attributed to Sigmund Freud."

He nods. "I majored in psychology."

I stifle my surprise. "You went to college?"

"What? You think a beach bum like me is automatically not educated?"

"No. I didn't mean—"

"That's exactly what you meant."

I sigh. He's right. I can't get out of this. "I'm sorry I misjudged you."

"University of Hawaii," he says. "Magna cum laude, even."

"Did you ever consider..."

"Doing something besides bartending? Of course I did. But I love what I do. I can live on the beach, make some great dough. Plus, I invested in a buddy's tech startup back in school. It gives me a nice little side income."

"Cool." Cool? *Really, Em?* He just told you he's not a beach bum loser, and you say cool?

"How about you? How'd you end up here, pretty girl?"

"I told you. A fellowship."

"I don't want the canned response. I want the truth."

My mouth drops open.

I want to tell him. I want to tell him everything. Dare I?

"Art school," I finally reply. "Art school at UCLA. I've sold a few pieces, but it takes a while to get a name in art, even in LA, where up-and-coming celebrities throw money at art—and new artists—just to look like they're cultured. So I wait tables on the side."

Not a total lie. That was my life *before* Lucifer.

"How old are you?" he asks.

"Twenty-six. You?"

"Twenty-five." He smiles. "That makes me your cub."

I smile despite myself. This man makes me feel good. Really good.

And boy, it's been a while since I've felt good.

"Sometimes a walk is just a walk," I say.

"True enough."

"So let's go." I grab his hand.

It's warm in mine.

And it feels nice. Really nice.

## 6

## SCOTTY

I'm not the kind of guy who wears his heart on his sleeve, or even believes in any of that mushy stuff, but damn... Em's hand in mine shoots a spark through me that I feel all the way to my toes. And specifically in one other place that's become pretty darned attentive at the moment.

"If you love the sunset from your lanai," I say, "you won't believe how gorgeous it is out here when we're walking on the beach."

Em looks to the west, where the sun is just getting ready to meet the horizon. "Tangerine. Sort of. With an element of fuchsia. How can the sun be a different color here?"

"Because there isn't any smog to take away from its beauty."

"I suppose, but I've been to Hawaii before. Sorry, but this is different."

"Parts of Hawaii are pretty industrialized," I tell her. "Honolulu, for example, and Hilo on the Big Island. Sure, you can probably see things a lot better than you can in LA, but this island is in a category of its own."

She sighs. "It sure is. When I see beauty like this..."

"What?"

"Oh, nothing."

"Come on. Tell me. This is a walk on the gorgeous beach at sunset. Almost a prerequisite to share your feelings."

She looks toward the west once more. "I almost feel like this place can absorb all the negativity in the world, you know? Like nothing bad can ever happen here."

I squeeze her hand. Clearly she doesn't know the history of this island. The Wolfe family covered it up as best they could, but some of us still got wind of it when we got here to begin work. I'm not going to be the one to shatter Em's illusions. No reason at all to tell her this island used to be a private resort where men could pay to hunt women as if they were prey. Where women were abducted and held captive and subjected to the sadistic fantasies of sociopathic multi-millionaires.

I say only, "It's a gorgeous place, for sure."

"It almost makes me feel..."

"...safe?" I finish for her.

She turns to me, her eyes troubled. "Yes, safe. But I mean that in a purely hypothetical way."

Sure, she does. I don't want to push, but I desperately want to know what Em's hiding. I want to help her, which is odd, as I barely know her. What is she running from? And why? Who would want to hurt this angel?

"Tell me something about yourself," I say. "Something no one else knows."

She wrinkles her brow. "Like what?"

"I don't know. I'm not asking for any deep, dark secret. Just something no one else knows about you. It can be a freckle on your ass, for all I care."

She rolls her eyes. "My ass is free from freckles, thanks."

"Something else, then."

She nods. "How about this? You go first, since this is your idea."

I inhale. "All right. I once had a threesome."

She laughs. "Only once?"

I stop walking. "Yeah, only once. Not exactly the reaction I expected."

"Most lotharios like you have had a few threesomes. It's the island mentality, right? Island time and all that?"

"First...lothario?"

"It means womanizer."

"I know what it means. Not a dumbass beach bum, remember? I just didn't realize we were in the nineteenth century. Also, it implies that I'm selfish in my seduction of women. I can assure you that isn't the case."

"Oh. I didn't mean to imply—"

"Actually, you did. You absolutely meant to imply that I'm some kind of ruthless seducer of women who cares only for his own pleasure. I guarantee you both the women in my threesome were well taken care of."

She's quiet for a moment, and she releases my hand. "I'm screwing this up, aren't I?"

I grab her hand again. "I think you deserve another chance."

"You're serious, then?"

"About only having one threesome? Of course."

"No, I mean you're serious that no one else knows you had the threesome? Because there are at least two others who know."

I can't help a laugh. "You're right. I did bend the rules. The two women know, but no one else does, at least not from me. I don't kiss and tell, despite what you may think about lotharios like me."

She looks down at the sand. "I shouldn't have said that."

"No, you shouldn't have. Look. I like women. I like sex. I'm not ashamed of that."

"I never said you should be."

"I suppose you didn't. Now, you owe me a response. Tell me something no one knows about you. Or no more than two people, I guess." I smiled.

She pauses a moment. Then, "No one knows I'm here."

"Here on the beach?"

"Here. On the island."

"Not true," I say. "*I* know you're here. Everyone else on the island knows you're here."

"I mean—"

I touch my finger to her lips. "Shh. I know what you mean. I know you're running, Em."

"I'm not—"

I cup her soft cheek and bring my lips to hers. Yes, I'm shutting her up, because she's lying to me and I don't want her to do that.

But I also desperately want to kiss her.

I slide my lips gently over hers, probing the seam with my tongue. A few seconds pass, but then she sighs and parts her lips.

I dive in, finding her silky tongue, and though I'm aching to kiss her deeply, I take it slowly and gently, melting into her mouth.

Yes, slow and sweet and—

She cups my cheeks harshly. *She* deepens the kiss. *Her*. Em.

I respond with vigor, delving as deeply as I can into her with my lips and tongue. She's warm and inviting, and she tastes like hamburgers and mint, which is suddenly my favorite flavor in the world.

And I realize I'll do anything to get this woman in my bed.

Tonight.

## 7

## EMILY

This kiss...

I knew it would happen. Expected it, even.

But this...

Scotty's kiss is unlike any other kiss I've experienced...and I've been with some expert kissers.

Scotty, though, has made kissing into an art—and I love art.

Not just painting, which is my preferred medium, but all art. Sculpture, poetry, music...and kissing.

His tongue is velvet against mine, his lips full and soft. I scrape my fingers over his dark stubble and then wrap my arms around his neck, pulling him closer to me.

Our bodies are melded together now, and my nipples harden, press into his chest. I kiss him more deeply, until—

He pulls away.

My fingers go absently to my lips. What just happened?

"My place?" he says.

He wants to get me in the sack. Of course he does. He's a beach bum lothario.

What's holding me back? Lucifer and I are over, despite what he thinks. And Scotty...

I want Scotty. If he's this good at kissing, he's got to be amazing at everything else.

My whole body is on fire, but, "I can't."

He nods. "I understand."

Except he doesn't. He thinks I don't want him. The fact is, I don't want to pull him into my drama.

Because Lucifer *will* find me.

It's only a matter of when.

This beautiful island may be off his radar for now, but he'll find it.

*You'll never escape me, Emily. You're mine. Mine to do with what I want.*

Even now, so close to Scotty, Lucifer's low voice haunts me.

Scotty grabs my hand. "I'll walk you back to your room."

"But..."

"But what?" He turns and meets my gaze.

My God, his eyes are something out of a Renaissance painting. Are they brown? Green? Golden? They change, according to the angle, according to the light.

"You promised me a walk on the beach. Or did you

really mean a walk to your bed?" I smile, hoping he can take the joke.

"I'm not going to lie, pretty girl. I want to make love to you. Desperately."

Desperately.

*I need you desperately, Emily.*

Lucifer was fond of that word.

"I didn't come here for that," I say.

"Why did you come here, then?"

"To paint," I say too quickly. "Why does anyone come here?"

He touches my cheek. Just a flutter of a touch, but I feel it intensely between my legs. A small sigh escapes my throat.

"I think it's more than that," Scotty says softly. "It's written all over your face. Your eyes, especially."

"Oh? What do you see in my eyes?"

"I see desire, Em. I see passion. But I also see fear."

"You can see all that? From a major in psychology?"

He trails his finger over the shell of my ear, pushing my hair back. "I can see all that because I'm interested in you. In what makes you tick."

"You're interested in getting me on my back," I say.

He chuckles, shaking his head. "You do have a one-track mind."

"*I* have a one-track mind? You already admitted it."

"I did, so why are you the one who keeps bringing it up?"

My cheeks burn. He makes a good point, which

pisses me off. Because the truth is, I want nothing more than to get between the sheets with this gold medal kisser. I want to lose myself in his magnificent body, underneath his magnificent tongue.

"Let's just finish our walk," I say, without looking into his eyes again.

Those eyes—they're hypnotic. If I look again, I fear I'll melt into a puddle of honey, and he'll scoop me up and take me to his place.

Which is what I want now more than my next breath of air.

"Good enough." He flips off his slides and picks them up. "Let's try the water."

I look down at my dress. "In this?"

"Just wading in the sand."

"What about jellyfish?"

"You see any?" He gestures.

I don't. Not like the beaches in LA sometimes. I've gotten used to always wearing flip-flops on the sand.

"The beach guys are good about letting us know if we need shoes. We haven't had a jellyfish invasion since I've been here."

I wiggle out of my flip-flops and step into the sand, letting it squish between my toes. I laugh. Actually laugh!

"What?" Scotty asks.

"It just feels good. Sand between my toes, like when I was a little kid. I'd almost forgotten."

"You're from the California coast, and you've

forgotten sand between your toes? We need to take care of that!"

I gasp as he swoops me into his arms and carries me toward the water. "What are you doing?"

"Showing you what's important in life."

Scotty carries me to the water's edge, but he keeps going. Soon he's nearly up to his knees in the water.

"You wouldn't," I say.

"Want to bet?"

In the next second, I'm tumbling into the water, splashing.

"That's a risky game," I say, spitting out salt water. "What if I couldn't swim?"

"The water's two feet deep, pretty girl. You aren't in any danger of drowning."

Except I am.

Scotty just doesn't know it.

## 8

## SCOTTY

Em looks far from happy. The dunking was a mistake.

A big one.

"Hey," I say, pushing her damp hair behind her ears. "I'm sorry."

"It's okay. You were just having fun."

"Yeah, the operative word being 'you.' I thought it'd be fun for both of us."

"How in the world is a dunking fun for me?" She shakes her head.

"Tell you what." I grin. "I'll dunk myself, and then we're even."

I dash into the water and dive in. Though the water's warm, it's still a welcome respite to the tropical humidity. It douses the perspiration from my body as I swim, the water so clear that I see the wonder of the Aquarian wildlife.

When I finally come up for air, I'm a good hundred feet away from shore.

I wave at Em, who looks gorgeous with her wet halter and skirt clinging to her amazing body.

She smiles.

And I feel like I've won the fucking lottery.

Does this mean she forgives me? I swim freestyle back to the shore.

She's laughing.

Nice.

Very nice.

"Are we even now?" I ask.

"Except you went into the water of your own volition," she says. "I didn't get a choice."

"I'd have let you throw me in, but I'm a little bit heavier than you are."

She shakes her head. "Is there anything you won't do?"

"A few things," I say.

"Like what?"

"Hmm... Here's a good one. I won't eat goat cheese."

"Yuck! Me neither."

"This is so meant to be," I tell her.

"Yeah, that's what I'm looking for in a man. A mutual hatred of goat cheese."

"You found him!"

She shakes her head, smiling again. Trying not to laugh. Her lips are quivering.

"Why, Em?" I ask.

"Why what?"

"Why are you so determined not to succumb to my obvious charms?"

She looks to the sky, smiling, and then she meets my gaze. "If only..."

"If only...what?" I narrow the distance between us, my toes sinking in the wet sand.

"Nothing."

I cup her cheek. Man, her skin is soft. Like freaking silk. "It's not nothing. Tell me."

"I hardly know you."

"You know about as much about me as anyone. More, even. Most people here don't know I went to college."

"Why not?"

"Because I don't talk about myself a lot."

Her eyebrows nearly fly off her forehead. "Really? You? A bartender? You haven't stopped talking since we met."

"It's what bartenders do, Em. We talk to customers about what they want to talk about, not about ourselves."

Her forehead wrinkles when I say Em.

"You don't like Em?" I say.

"I like it, actually," she says. "My brother calls me Em."

"You have a brother, then?"

"Yeah. Just one. No sisters."

"What's his name?"

"Buck. Buck Moreno."

"So he's a half-brother, then?"

"No, why?"

I grin. "I thought your last name was Smith. Don't tell me you're married!"

She reddens. I mean *really* reddens. Like I totally want to see how far down that rosiness goes.

"Not married," she says. "Divorced."

"Ah..." I smile.

I'm not buying that lie either, but I'll let her remain a mystery for a few more minutes.

But only a few more minutes.

Because after those minutes pass, I'm going to kiss her again. Then I'm going to take her to my hut and fuck her silly.

If there was ever a woman who needed a good fuck, it's Emily Smith Moreno.

"Scotty..." she begins.

"Yeah?"

"I'm not divorced."

I drop my jaw in mock surprise.

"And my name is Emily Moreno, not Emily Smith."

"You've been lying to me?" More mock surprise. "Not just about Portland and your last name?"

"Yeah, but I have reasons. Really good reasons."

"Which are...?"

"I can't tell you," she says. "I can only tell you that it has nothing to do with you. I...like you."

"I like you too, Em." I thumb her lower lip. "And you can tell me. You can trust me."

She scoffs softly. "I've been burned by those words before."

"By the person you're hiding from?"

She bites her lower lip then. "I have to go. Back to the hut. I'm… I'm tired."

I should let her go.

She's got baggage, this one, and if there's one thing a beach bum like me doesn't need, it's baggage. I love the carefree life. I love being as free as the soft wind that blows on the island.

I love my life.

*Right. Let her go, Scotty. Let. Her. Go.*

I grip her shoulders and kiss her again.

## 9

## EMILY

His lips are so firm on mine, and again, I want to give in to the kiss, let him take me away and forget everything I'm dealing with.

His tongue tangles with mine as he deepens the kiss, and a raw growl emanates from his chest into mine.

How easy it would be to allow this... To fully escape the ties that bind me to LA.

To Lucifer Black.

What if Buck can't stop him?

What if he finds me?

Buck has the Wolfes behind him, But Lucifer...

Lucifer has his father's money—not Wolfe money by a long shot, but still enough to do as he chooses. And Lucifer has something the Buck and the Wolfes don't have.

He's obsessed with me.

He'll do anything to get me back.

All my energy is required to push Scotty away. Our kiss breaks with a pop of suction.

His green-gold eyes are burning. On fire, even. They pierce me, and I swear I can feel the scorch on my flesh.

"Em..." he growls.

"I'm sorry, Scotty. I'm so sorry." I turn and run away from him.

Or attempt to. Running on sand is difficult. I should be used to it, being from LA beach country, but I nearly stumble.

Scotty catches up to me, grabs my shoulders again, and whips me around to face him.

"Em," he says, "you've got to let me help you."

"You can't help me." I wipe what might turn into a tear away from my eye. "No one can."

"You're wrong."

I look to the sky, dragging my fingers through my tangled hair. "God, I wish I were!"

He cups my cheek, rubbing his thumb over my bottom lip again. Just his touch sends me reeling. Such a loving touch—a touch meant to spark desire in me.

It does that and more.

"What if I stop the lothario routine," he says. "What if I take you to my place and we talk. Just talk."

I can't help myself. I roll my eyes. "You've been coming on to me all evening, and you think I'm going to fall for the 'let's just talk' line? I'm not that innocent or gullible, Scotty."

He gazes at me, and his eyes—those gorgeous eyes—

narrow slightly. Only slightly, and his lips curve downward.

Is he upset? Upset that he won't be bedding me, most likely.

"Em," he says, "it's not a line. I want to help, but it's clear that you don't want my help. I'll walk you back to your hut."

"It's okay," I say. "Please. I don't want to be any more of a spectacle than I've already made myself." I walk off the beach and onto the boardwalk that leads to the colonists' huts.

I don't expect him to follow me. It's still light out, and this place is safe anyway.

At least until Lucifer finds me.

I get to my hut and unlock the door. As I walk in, I look over my shoulder.

Scotty is ten feet away.

He *did* follow me. He sure was quiet about it. It was sweet, too, for him to make sure I got back safely while honoring my request not to be a spectacle.

Walking with the best-looking man on this island would definitely make me a spectacle.

Being a spectacle is not a good way to stay invisible.

Not a good way at all.

*Buck taught me how to pick locks when I was sixteen. He's six years older than I am, and he'd just returned from Navy*

*SEAL training. I remember being surprised at how simple it was.*

*"Practice," Buck said. "Practice a lot until it's second nature to you. You never know when you might need the skill." He gave me a lock-picking wrench before he left for his first assignment.*

*I no longer had the lock-picking kit. I lost it on the beach one day when I was showing it to a friend. Just as well. If I'd had it when I hooked up with Lucifer, he'd have found it when he confiscated all my stuff. Then he'd have known I could pick locks.*

*That's how I escaped from Lucifer.*

*It was simple luck that he forgot to turn the deadbolt that day. I'd stolen a couple paperclips from a pile of documents several weeks earlier, and I'd pretty much given up hope.*

*Until that day.*

*That day when he forgot to lock the deadbolt.*

*I knew as soon as he left.*

*The soft click of the lock on the doorknob, and then the louder click of the deadbolt.*

*Only the soft click that day.*

*The lock I could easily pick.*

*I waited a few minutes. I had to make sure he was gone. But after twenty minutes passed, I didn't dare wait any longer. I had no idea when he'd come back, and I wanted to be long gone by then.*

*I straightened the paperclips each into one long wire and began.*

*I inserted one wire into the bottom of the keyhole and*

*applied a little pressure. The other went in at the top of the keyhole. I scrubbed the top wire back and forth while I applied more pressure. My heart jumped when the first pin clicked into place.*

*Ten minutes later, I turned the doorknob.*

*I was familiar with Lucifer's place. It was a beachfront house on a private beach with lots of security.*

*Security wasn't a problem for me either. I'd spent the last several weeks studying the system. Lucifer never let me watch when he keyed in the code, but each number had a certain sound. I'd memorized the sounds and the position of his hands.*

*Yeah, that's how badly I wanted out of there.*

*This man.*

*This man who, when I met him, I thought could be the one.*

*He was gorgeous and brilliant and rich.*

*He was also domineering and arrogant and tyrannical.*

*He was born into money, but once I got deep into his world, I found out he didn't depend on family money.*

*Lucifer made his money in drugs.*

*The underground drug trade on the streets of LA.*

*Once I knew too much, he started locking me up.*

*"It's because I love you," he'd say. "I want to keep you safe."*

*I believed him at first. Actually believed him! I was clouded by lust and by love.*

*Once he realized he could control me, he became even more autocratic.*

*Though he denied it, I was essentially his slave.*

*Now, I was free!*

*I disarmed the security system and left the house.*

*I left the house!*

*The first time I'd left the place without Lucifer since I moved in over a year prior.*

*I had no phone, no money, and only the clothes on my back.*

*But I had the will. The will to escape.*

*I also knew how to get off the property without being seen. I'd studied the video feeds Lucifer kept.*

*I knew how to get off his property undetected.*

*Once I was safely off his land, I found a crowded beach where no one would recognize me.*

*A lovely woman with two kids lounged near the lifeguard.*

*"Excuse me, ma'am. I'm so sorry, but my purse got stolen, and I need to call my brother to come get me. Could I borrow your phone?"*

*"Of course." She smiled and handed me her cell phone.*

*"Thank you. I'll only be a minute." I walked away so I could talk in private.*

*One call.*

*To Buck.*

*That's all it took.*

*Three hours later, I was on a plane to Billionaire Island.*

## 10

## SCOTTY

I followed her.

This island is safe, but still... She's so scared of something or someone, so I wanted to make sure she got to her hut safely.

Damn.

Horny and off the clock. Not such a problem when you're on an island of lovelies.

Except only one woman invades my mind.

Em, with her long dark hair, her searing brown eyes, her milky skin.

Normally I'd hang at the beach or at the bar, people watching, conversing, probably picking up a woman. Usually a staffer. Bedding the art colonists is pretty frowned upon, though I'll admit I've done it a time or two. Or three.

My buddy Lyle is tending bar, so I pony up and take the last available stool next to Nemo, our server from the burger bar. He and Lyle are also my roommates. Well, not roommates so much as suitemates. Staffers share huts, but we each have our own bedroom, which is cool. I'm four years out of college and totally over the "hang a sock on the door if you've got a girl inside" days.

Lyle's a blond surfer boy from LA but Nemo's half Hawaiian like I am. He looks the part more than I do, though—black hair and dark brown eyes, tan skin. I got my dad's hazel eyes and slightly fairer skin. The three of us have kind of become known among the staffers as the Island lotharios, to use Em's word.

"You too, Scotty?" Lyle says, sliding an ice water in front of me. "What are the two most eligible beach bums doing here at the bar when you could be hooking up? What happened to that gorgeous hunkette you were with when you got off duty?"

"She's tired. Went back to her hut."

Lyle erupts into boisterous laughter. "You couldn't seal the deal, huh?"

"You mean the chick you had dinner with?" Nemo asks. "Man, she's a hottie."

A hottie? A hunkette? Words I've used to describe women many times, but coming from the mouths of Lyle and Nemo, they seem immature and patronizing. I vow never to use them again.

"She's got class," I say.

"Too much class to hook up with the likes of you, huh?" Nemo punches my upper arm.

I love these guys, I do, but man, are hookups all they think about?

I can't escape the irony of my thought.

Hookups are all I thought about until this evening. In fact, I was damned determined to get Em between the sheets.

I let her go.

Sure, I can say it was her obvious baggage, and that's probably part of it.

But it's way more than that.

I let her needs take precedence over my own. She wasn't ready to be with me, so I let her go. I didn't press her. Normally, I press a little more. I never force a woman, of course, but I can be very persuasive.

"Her name's—" I stop.

She's hiding. She probably doesn't want her name spread everywhere.

"What?" Nemo asks. "What's her name?"

"She wouldn't tell me."

"Easy enough to find out. I can get the guest list from Manuel. Which hut is she in?"

For God's sake. He's right. Any staffer can find out who she is. "Emily," I say. "Her name's Emily. And the two of you keep your hands to yourselves."

"Why the 'she wouldn't tell me' thing, then?" Nemo asks.

"She's trying to keep to herself," I say. "I don't want you guys bugging her."

"Dude," Lyle says, "if you like her, we'll stay away. Buddies' rule book and all. Bros before hoes."

"Would you stop saying that?" I give him an evil eye. "It's degrading."

"I gotta agree, Lyle," Nemo adds.

"Okay, okay." Lyle straightens his posture. "Buds before chicks. Is that better?"

"Slightly," I say. "Not really."

"You've got it bad," Lyle says, mixing a drink for a colonist. "Friends before women. Does that work for you?"

I take a sip of water. "I do like her. Thanks."

"I'm off in thirty," Lyle says. "Siri and Angel are having a beach party on the staffer beach. Somehow they got their hands on a couple kegs. We should go."

"That's where I'm headed," Nemo agrees.

"A kegger, guys? Really?" I shake my head.

"Since when are you too good for a kegger?"

"I'm not. It's just..."

"It's just your fantasy woman won't be there," Nemo says. "Am I right?"

"So invite her," Lyle says.

"To a staff party? I don't think so. I don't need to get my ass fired for fraternizing."

"You already had dinner with her," Nemo reminds me.

Good point. We're actually supposed to mingle with the guests. It's encouraged. Roy and Charlie Wolfe want this place to seem like a home away from home for the artists. A place where they can study their craft and also have a luxury island experience. Meet people, know the staff members who are helping to make their stay comfortable.

No one brings colonists to the staff parties, though.

"Nah," I say. "I'll bach it with you two tonight."

Siri Campbell and Angel Akina are lifeguards at the beach. Excellent swimmers, both of them, so they have rocking bodies. We call them night and day. Siri was born in Jamaica and has gorgeous dark skin and hair, and Angel, despite her Hawaiian last name, is blond and fair.

And of course they're both knockouts.

Lyle and Nemo have sampled Siri and Angel, respectively.

I haven't yet had the pleasure.

Siri, clad in a white bikini that accentuates her gorgeous brown skin, is the first to welcome me.

"Scotty!" She grabs me in a hug and shoves a red plastic cup containing beer in my hand. "Good to see you!"

"You see me every day, Siri."

"Yeah," she laughs, "and it's always good! Welcome to our kegger!"

"Thanks."

"I can't believe Angel got her hands on these kegs,"

Siri continues. "Her cousin is a distributor, and he sneaked a few extra into the last shipment."

"Lucky break," I say.

"Isn't it?" She gulps a swallow of beer. "Have a good time!" She flits away and joins another group of staffers.

I watch her. Siri Campbell has the best ass on the beach.

Except maybe for Emily's ass, which I've only seen with a wet skirt clinging to it.

It was *fine*.

Lyle and Nemo are already in party mode and making the rounds. Normally I'd be with them, but something holds me back tonight.

Not something so much as some*one*.

Within two minutes, though, Nemo finds me and drags me into the circle where he and Lyle are holding court with a bevy of female staffers, Lauren Suvac among them. Lauren's another bartender, and she and I hooked up once. Nothing serious. She's a gorgeous blonde with massive tits and a cute spray of freckles across her nose.

"Hey, Scotty." She puts her hand in mine. "How's it hanging tonight?"

"Good, Laur. How about you?"

"Feeling kind of lonely." She squeezes my hand. "And horny."

Yeah. Normally I'd be all over that. Lauren's great, because she was an anthropology major in college. She doesn't believe in monogamy. "There's just no science to support it," she told me once. "Most mammalian species never form monogamous relationships. They have different partners for different times in their lives."

Yeah. I kissed her to get her to shut up.

Funny.

Monogamy doesn't sound quite so bad to me tonight.

"You interested?" She tugs on my hand.

"Maybe later." I kiss her cheek quickly. "Want to take a swim?"

"Sure! Last one in the water's a rotten egg!" She peels off her fire-engine red one piece and runs into the ocean in her birthday suit.

So it's that kind of party, huh? I disrobe quickly as well and follow her into the water. It's warm, and the sun has fallen below the horizon, casting a blue veil over everything. Lauren's huge tits float on the water and draw my gaze.

But...

Been there, done that.

I dive under for a minute, let the water cover my body. When I reappear, Lauren has set her sights on Nemo, who's joined us in the water.

Just as well. Nemo needs to get laid, and Lauren's a sure thing.

I, on the other hand?

I don't *need* to get laid. However, I desperately *want* to get laid. By Emily Moreno.

I get out of the water and grab a towel from the stack

Siri and Angel provided. I dry off my hair, wrap the towel around my waist, and go in search of my clothes.

Siri grabs one of my butt cheeks. "Best ass on the beach, Scotty."

"Yours is better."

She laughs. "Lyle took an informal poll at the bar tonight. You won best guy ass and I won best girl ass."

"I can't find any fault with those results."

"You want to roast marshmallows?" Siri asks. "We started a small bonfire. Got everything for s'mores."

"Sure. What the hell?" I hastily get back into my shorts and island shirt and follow Siri to the small fire.

We're allowed to have a bonfire, but only in this one location on the staffers' beach. The Wolfes are great to all of us. Our own private beach, great living quarters, all food and drink included. I guess that makes up for the meager pay. No tips, either. It's forbidden. The artists are here to create, not go broke. Roy Wolfe's words. Of course, a few of them still tip. Lyle and I learned quickly who they were and we give them extra special service.

Still we make enough to get by and put a few bucks each check into savings. With shelter, food, and drink included here, it's an amazing deal. I was lucky I got hired on Billionaire Island. I take a roasting fork and load it with two marshmallows. Angel and Lyle are among the others around the small fire. Siri and I join them.

"You got any dark chocolate?" I ask Siri.

"Sure thing. I remember you don't eat Hershey's."

"Tastes like sour milk to me," I say.

"I got you some Special Dark."

"You're awesome!" I give Siri a kiss on her smooth cheek.

Funny. I've kissed two women's cheeks tonight. Lauren and Siri. And I felt nothing. Not even a slight stir downstairs.

I'm off my game.

Except I know I'm not.

I'm *on* my game. Totally on it.

I just have my sights set on another woman.

Once my marshmallows are brown but not burnt, I move them from the fire and slide them onto a graham cracker along with a square of dark chocolate. I top it with another graham cracker, and just as I'm about to shove it into my mouth—

I shift my gaze toward the other side of the beach.

Darkness has fallen, and a lone woman wanders barefoot, right at the shoreline. She's dressed all in white —a sundress—dark hair falling down her back.

An angel.

A fucking angel on the beach.

I absently drop my s'more in the sand and begin walking.

## 11

## EMILY

I feel safer in the dark.

Silly, I know.

If Lucifer wants to find me—and he does—he will. Eventually. Buck will do what he can to throw him off my trail, but in the end...

He'll find me.

*You're mine, Emily. You'll never escape me.*

This is the edge of the colonists' beach. A fire burns in the distance. I inhale. Mmm. Smells like campfire and roasted marshmallows. S'mores.

I haven't had a s'more since I was a little girl. I used to be a Girl Scout. Emily Moreno was a good girl. She was always prepared—the Girl Scout motto. She earned good grades and never got into trouble.

Never.

Until she met Lucifer Black.

I'm an accessory to myriad crimes, now. Not by my

choice, but that won't matter to the people who want to bring down Lucifer and his underground syndicate.

I know too much, as well.

Which is why Lucifer can't let me go.

Security here on the island is top notch, according to Buck. He should know. He's been in the Wolfes' employ since he left the Navy. He and his friend Leif are two of the Wolfes' hired guns, so to speak. They're jacks of all trades with a SEAL background. I don't even want to think about some of the stuff my brother most likely did when the Wolfes were all suspects in their father's murder.

Thankfully, that's all over now. Turned out Derek Wolfe had led a double life. He was a bigamist, a kidnapper, a rapist, and a psychopath.

Nice guy.

The ocean pushes toward me, tickling my bare toes.

I let out a sigh.

I'm in paradise.

Paradise.

And earlier today, I met a man. A nice man who seemed interested in me. Wanted to know why I'm running. Why I'm hiding. Sure, he's a bartending beach bum, but I liked him. I wanted to get to know him.

Wanted...

Wanted to feel his strong arms around me.

But I couldn't. It wouldn't be fair to him, when I belong to someone else.

Except I don't belong to someone else. Damn.

Lucifer's words haunt me to the point where I actually believe them sometimes.

No. I do *not* belong to Lucifer Black.

I belong only to me.

But he will come for me.

And I can't bear the thought of Scotty being in his way. If Scotty got hurt because of me, I'd never forgive myself.

The water meets my toes once more, this time more forceful, and the water flows up to my ankles, burying the gold anklet. Then just as quickly, the water flows back out to sea, leaving my feet buried in the wet sand.

Buried.

I'm like my feet, in a way. Buried. I so want to climb out of Lucifer's grasp, but I know my time here on Wolfe Island is only a temporary respite.

He's coming.

I can feel it.

"Hey, pretty girl."

I jolt at the words and look up. Scotty's walking toward me carrying two red plastic cups. He hands me one.

"Brought you a drink."

I look into the cup and sniff. "Beer?"

"You too good for beer, pretty girl?"

"No. It's just been...a long time since I've had a beer." I take drink, letting the cold maltiness coat my mouth and throat. I swallow. "It's good."

"It's basic Bud Light. The stuff of frat parties."

"Still, it's good. Refreshing."

He takes a swallow. "It is that. Nothing like the Scotty special, though, right?"

I smile. "That was in a class by itself."

"You come up with a name yet?"

"Not yet." I take another sip of beer.

"We've got time."

"I suppose." Except he's wrong. There's an invisible timer around my neck. I'm just not sure when it's set to expire.

"You want to come to a party?"

"Your bonfire?"

"Yeah. It's a staff party, but I bet they'll let you in." He points. "That's our beach over there. For staff use only. It's really nice."

"If it's for staff use only, I shouldn't go over there. I don't want to get anyone in trouble."

"You won't, but I get it." He smiles and pushes a lock of hair out of my eye. "Will I see you tomorrow?"

"I don't know. I may not leave my hut."

"Emily," he says.

And I listen. I listen because he's never called me Emily before. Either pretty girl or Em.

Never Emily.

"...you're on a beautiful island. You can paint to your heart's content. That's why you're here. But I'm not going to let you waste your time here by sitting alone in your hut every day until you leave.

"I—"

"Look." He grabs both my hands.

Tingles shoot through me.

"I won't force you to do anything. I don't have that power over you and I don't want it. But whatever you're hiding from, it won't find you here. I promise you."

I can't help it. I shake my head and let out a scoffing laugh. "You just don't know."

"I'll know if you tell me."

I meet his gorgeous gaze. "Nice try."

"You don't have to tell me anything. In fact, we don't have to go back to the staff party. We can walk along the shoreline, as you've been doing. Or I can leave you here. You can walk alone. It's safe."

"I don't want to keep you from your party."

"I'd much rather have your company. May I walk with you?"

I nod. He drops one of my hands and we begin walking, hand in hand, in the opposite direction, away from the staffer beach and his party.

Toward the colony, the bar, the restaurants. We walk past the people who are out painting in the dark, past the couples chatting intimately, past the night lifeguard on duty, past the surf and rent shop.

Past everything, until the shoreline and the moon are our only company.

And my hand is still in his.

And I like the way it feels.

I like it very much.

I almost feel...*safe*.

## 12

## SCOTTY

I'm a bartender, which means I'm a talker. It also means I can recognize when a customer doesn't want to talk. If I talk too much to someone who doesn't want it, I don't get a tip—at least at bars where tipping is allowed. It's all about reading people.

I'm reading Em now. She doesn't want to talk.

That's okay.

Sure, I want to know more about her. Man, I want to know everything about her, but in her time.

I don't know how long she's booked here on the island. I could check with Manual, but does it matter?

I'm a live-for-the-day kind of guy. *Carpe diem* and all that. I always have been, and today's no different.

Perhaps Emily will leave tomorrow. Perhaps she'll stay a couple months.

All that matters is this moment. Right now.

And although I won't deny that I'd love to get her

between the sheets, I'm content, in this moment, to walk to along the shoreline with her and simply hold her hand.

So I'm surprised when she stops walking and turns to face the ocean.

"It's so vast," she says. "I can see so far just in the moonlight."

"The moon doesn't actually make any light," I say. "It's a reflection from the sun."

She smiles. "You learned that as a psychology major?"

"No, I learned that in seventh-grade earth science."

She laughs. Just a slight laugh, but it's beautiful. It's joyous. It makes a grin split my face.

"You're something, Emily Moreno."

"Am I?" Her tone is slightly flirtatious.

I trail a finger over her soft cheek, down her neck. "You definitely are." I lean in and give her a chaste kiss on the lips.

I pull back, but shock rolls through me as Em wraps her arms around my neck and pulls me into a clench, crushing our mouths together.

Unexpected...and awesome.

Her soft lips slide against mine, her tongue probes mine.

Em is taking charge of this kiss. Very different from our previous kisses, and I'm loving it. Really loving it.

I glide one hand down her shoulder to her breasts, resisting the urge to cup one. Instead, I slide my hand down her waist to her hips and around to one of her ass cheeks. I pull her toward me, let her feel my hard cock against her belly.

Then she unclenches herself from my grasp.

*I'm sorry*. The words are on the tip of my tongue, but I can't bring myself to say them. I'm not sorry. Not sorry at all.

I want more kisses. I want more than kisses. I want to make love to Em, hard and fast, and then slowly and passionately.

But I won't pressure her.

"I'm sorry." The words I considered saying come from her lips instead of mine.

"Don't be," I say. "Never be sorry. If you're not feeling what I'm feeling—"

She shakes her rapidly. "I am. I'm feeling exactly what you're feeling, Scotty. I swear it."

I inhale. I love the smell of the beach at night. Sand and saltwater and shells, but tonight, I get a waft of Emily's citrusy perfume, her coconutty hair, her...sultry musk.

Yeah, I can smell her need. Her ache. Her want.

It mirrors my own.

Should I ask her if she wants to go to my hut?

No. She stopped the kiss. She wants me and I want her, but she stopped me from going any further.

"You want to walk back?" I ask.

She breathes in and reaches both arms out, as if sizing up her wingspan. She faces the ocean, closes her eyes, inhales again. “This place makes me think anything is possible.”

I want so badly to touch her, to kiss her, just to grab her hand even.

But I don’t.

I can’t.

I can’t disturb the picture she makes as she faces the sea, her eyes closed, her arms stretched out, her hair curtaining down her back, and her white dress flowing around her body in the soft evening breeze.

So I watch her. Take in the perfect embodiment of beauty before my eyes.

And I’m not sure I’ll ever tire of gazing at her.

## 13

## EMILY

The breeze on my flesh, the oceanic fragrance, the warmth of Scotty's body... We're not touching, but still, his presence invades me even as my eyes are closed. The flimsy fabric of my dress grazes my bare legs, the water tickles my toes.

And if I open my eyes, I'll see the moonlight streaming onto the midnight blue sea.

So lovely.

I expect Scotty to say something. Or to touch me. Kiss me.

But he doesn't.

He lets me be. Simply be.

Which comforts me.

He said I was safe here.

He's wrong, but I am at least safe for this moment.

I open my eyes, turn to face him.

He's gorgeous in the moonlight. It glints off his dark hair, creates a black veil over most of the colors in his clothing, but not his eyes. Not those olive-gold orbs that nearly seduced me the first time I gazed into them.

The darkness doesn't affect them at all.

"You're beautiful," he says, his low voice even lower than normal.

I take a step toward him, my feet sinking in the sand. "So are you."

He smiles. A wide smile that shows his sparkling white teeth against the dark of night.

"Will you do something for me?" I ask.

"Anything."

"Take me somewhere. Take me somewhere on this island where you've never taken another woman."

He widens his eyes, and for a moment, I fear a place like that doesn't exist on the island.

I try to hide my frown.

He grabs hold of my left hand, entwines my fingers through this. "I know just the place. Are you up for a little danger?"

I hold back a scoff. I'm in danger just by existing. "What kind of danger?"

"There's a cliff about a mile up the beach. It's off limits to colonists and staffers. My buddies and I visited it once."

"What's so dangerous about it? Is it high?"

"No. Not at all. But parts of it are covered in coral,

which can cut you up pretty badly, and neither of us is wearing shoes. But I'm not suggesting we actually get on the cliff."

"Why are you suggesting it, then?"

"Because right before we get to the cliff is a gorgeous stretch of beach. The sand is snow white, and the sunsets and sunrises are glorious."

"So you've been there with your friends..."

"I have. Nemo and Lyle. My suitemates." He smiles. "But I've never taken a woman there."

"Why not?"

"I've never wanted to."

"Wait, wait, wait. You went there with guys, and you say it's a gorgeous stretch of beach, but you never went back with a woman?"

"I never did."

"Why?" I can't help asking.

"It's too special," he says. "I never wanted to share it with a woman. Until now."

His words melt the last layer of ice around my heart. Lucifer Black disappears, and for this moment, I'm safe.

Safe with Scotty.

And I want to share this with him.

"Let's go," I say.

We walk another mile or so until I see the cliff he's talking about in the distance. "Beyond the cliff is the other side of the island. There's a retreat center there, and beyond that, the Wolfes are building a huge resort."

I nod. "My brother told me all about it."

"Oh?"

"Yeah. He works for the Wolfes."

Scotty nods. "I may apply for a job at the resort. Resorters are allowed to tip."

I laugh. "You're hardly living in poverty here."

"Not at all. But a guy's got to plan for the future."

I widen my eyes. Scotty is so much more than a beach bum. He's thinking about his future. I like that.

"I'm sorry," I say.

"For what?"

"For thinking you were a beach bum with no goals."

He stops walking. "That's what you thought?"

"Well, if it looks like a duck..."

"Hey." He cups my cheek. "I live day to day. I pull each sliver of happiness I can out of each minute of my day. But that doesn't mean I don't think about the future. In fact..."

"In fact...what?"

"In fact, I've been thinking more about the future during the last twelve hours than I have in a long time."

I don't reply. Does he mean me? Silly to even think that. We hardly know each other.

Still, his words warm me. Soothe me. Comfort me.

And, of course, turn me on.

The night is warm, and the ocean breeze cushions us. This tiny stretch of beach is isolated, pure white sand. What must a sunrise look like from here? A sunset?

I need to come back here with my paints.
But for now...
“Scotty?”
“Hmm?” He plays with my fingers.
“Kiss me. Please.”

## 14

## SCOTTY

I press my lips to hers gently. Oh, I'm raring to go. I'll gladly kiss her into tomorrow, but I get the impression she needs slow tonight.

So I gently pry her lips open with my tongue, delve between them, explore her mouth languidly.

She kisses me back, and then, to my surprise, she takes the lead.

She deepens the kiss, exploring my mouth this time, and tiny little groans vibrate from her throat into me, fueling my desire even more.

I grab a fist full of her long glorious hair and give it a sharp tug. She responds by grabbing my ass and pulling me closer to her.

The kiss, the beach, the world... It's all perfect.

I want her so badly. I haven't wanted a woman this badly in a long time, perhaps not ever.

She breaks the kiss and gasps in a breath. I inhale as well, trailing kisses across her cheek to her ear.

"You're so beautiful, Em," I whisper.

She shudders beneath my touch. "I wish..." she says.

"You wish what?"

"I wish we could stay here. Just you and me. Where there aren't any other cares in the world."

"We can." I nip at the outer shell of her soft ear.

"Mmm...we can't. The carriage will turn into a pumpkin eventually."

"But we don't have to think about that right now."

"But..." She sighs, trailing her fingers up my arms. "But...it always happens. It's inevitable."

"Shhhh," I say. "It won't happen tonight."

I ease her onto the soft sand until she's lying on her back, her dark eyes glowing in the moonlight. I've never seen anything lovelier. We're close to the shoreline but still on dry sand.

I kiss her again, deeply, our tongues tangling, our lips sliding, and then I work a strap of her white flowing dress.

She doesn't stop me.

Soon her breasts are bared, and my God, in the moonlight, I swear she's a goddess. Aphrodite herself. So beautiful and perfect, her nipples brown and hard and tight. I brush my fingers over one and then the other.

Then I lean down and take one between my lips.

She moans softly, so I suck harder, gripping the hard nub with my teeth and biting gently.

"Mmmm… Good, Scotty."

Very good from where I am as well. I cup the other breast and lightly thumb the nipple. I could spend hours on these gorgeous tits alone, but there's a certain heaven between her legs that calls me.

I let go of her breasts for a second—she whimpers—and remove my shirt. My dick is aching inside my board shorts, but I don't want to scare her off. I'll leave it encased for now.

But her dress. The top of it is bunched around her slender waist, while the bottom of it is still covering the gems between her legs.

I ease it over her hips.

And suck in a breath of air.

She's not wearing panties.

Nothing. Not ever a tiny lace thong. Her pussy is shaved clean, and her clit is glistening.

Oh. My. God.

I quickly ease the dress off her legs until it's sitting next to us in a puddle of white.

"Commando," I say huskily.

"I'd already showered. Thought I was going to bed, but then something called to me."

"What?"

"The ocean, I think. Or maybe…"

"Maybe what?"

"I think maybe it was you, Scotty."

I smile, glide my finger across her lower lip. "You think?"

"I suppose it sounds silly."

"Not silly to me. I think I made it pretty clear I wanted to spend more time with you."

"You did. But...I have no right to drag you into something I can't finish."

"Baby," I say, "all we need to think about finishing is tonight." I kiss her again. Hard.

She wraps her arms around me, and I roll on top of her, bracing myself so I don't crush her. She's naked beneath me, the sand cushioning us. My dick prods through my board shorts. Her pussy—only the thin fabric of my shorts separates my dick from her honey.

"Em..."

"Hmmm..."

"Tell me to stop now. Please. If you can't go through with this, you have to tell me now."

"Don't stop," she says on a breath. "Please don't stop. Take me, Scotty. Take me away from the cruel world."

"I'm not an escape, Em. But I can take you away for this moment." I move off of her quickly, remove my shorts, grab a condom out of my pocket, and sheath myself.

Then I move on top of her once more. "You sure?" I ask.

"Yes, Scotty. Please."

I thrust into her heat.

A groan begins deep in my soul and flows outward as I cushion myself within Emily's tight pussy.

My God.

It's like she was made for me.

Every other woman I've ever had suddenly disappears from my mind.

There's only Em. My wonderful pretty girl. Em. Emily.

Emily Moreno.

And I vow, as soon as I plunge into her, that I'll keep her safe.

Safe from whatever she's running from.

Safe from whatever she's hiding.

Safe.

Safe and comforted in my arms.

I pull out, thrust back in. Pull out, thrust back in.

"Scotty," she gasps. "Please. Scotty, please."

I thrust again and again, kneeing into the sand. "Em. God, you feel good."

"So long," she breathes. "It's been so long since I've felt so... Felt so... Ah!" She clamps around my dick.

God, a woman's climax never felt so good.

"That's it, baby. Come. Come for me."

She shrieks, but it doesn't matter. No one can hear us all the way out here.

"That's it," I say. "Keep coming. Keep coming."

*Thrust.*

*Thrust.*

*Thrust.*

And—

"Fuck!" I clench my teeth as I release inside her warmth.

Each pulse sends a quiver through my heart, through my soul.

And I wonder…

I wonder…if I'll ever feel this whole again.

## 15

## EMILY

I'm lost.

So lost in a sea of pleasure and happiness.

In the air, the breeze blows around us, and the sea roars in the distance, until—

"Oh!" The ocean rolls toward us, envelops us in the warm Pacific saltwater.

"Wow," Scotty says. "I couldn't have planned that any better."

I laugh, though I'm still quivering from the best orgasm I've ever experienced.

Is it the tropical island? Is it the man above me? Is it the fact that we just acted out a scene in *From Here to Eternity* with perfection?

Is it the fact that I'm running?

Probably a little of each.

Mostly it's Scotty.

Scotty, who gave me comfort. Who let me decide.

Who let me escape, if only for a few timeless moments, into his world of joy and lovemaking and tropical breezes.

"I don't want to move from this place," I say. "Not ever."

"No need to be in any hurry," he says.

"You have to work in the morning."

"That's still a few hours from now."

"What about sleep?"

"Sleep? Who needs it? I'll forgo sleep for the rest of your stay if it means I get to spend every minute with you."

*Nice line.*

I don't say it.

Because it's not a line. Scotty is sincere. I don't know how I know, but I do.

This man won't harm me.

Sure, it's an island fling.

It's not forever.

But it's now.

And now is all that matters.

We watch the sun rise together. If only I had my palette and a canvas. The blues and oranges and yellows and purples spiral together in a kaleidoscope of color as the sun eases over the horizon, hazing through a few scattered clouds that look like white cotton candy.

"I hate to be a party pooper," Scotty says, "but we're going to need some hydration.

He's not wrong. Even in this tropical humidity, I'm feeling dry. The last thing I drank was the beer several hours ago, and that was hardly thirst quenching.

I sigh. "I don't want to leave."

"We can come back tonight."

"Can we?"

"Of course! You think I'm letting you go after that? Tell me it was as mind-numbing for you as it was for me."

"More," I say.

He chuckles and cups my cheek. "We'll call it a tie, then."

"A tie." I close my eyes and breath in the fresh morning air. "I'm not sure I can move."

"Then I'll carry you. But I won't let you die of dehydration. Or starvation." He makes it to his feet and holds out his hand.

"Scotty?"

"Yeah?"

"If you didn't have to work today, would you stay here with me forever?"

He chuckles again. "Baby, I'd stay here as long as you want. But eventually we'd both need water."

I grab his hand and he pulls me into a stand and

then into his bare chest. Scotty's shirt and shorts are a couple yards away, but…

"Scotty? Where's my dress?"

He glances around. "Should be right here somewhere. Oh, crap."

"What?"

"It may have gotten washed out to sea when the tide came in and covered us."

My jaw drops. "How am I going to get back?'

He hastily pulls his shorts over his amazing ass and hands his shirt to me. "This should cover everything that needs covering."

I laugh.

I can't help it. I give a fucking loud laugh.

And I wish this moment could last forever.

I drape Scotty's shirt over my naked body and button it up. Sure enough, it covers my ass…but just barely. Still, it's good enough to get back to the colony and to my hut. And the best part? It smells just like Scotty—an intoxicating combination of the bonfire, the beach, and his spicy, masculine scent.

We walk, hand in hand, a little more quickly than I'd prefer because Scotty has to get to his morning shift at the bar. We arrive just in time for him to begin his shift.

"Don't you need your shirt?" I ask.

"Won't be the first time I've tended bar topless." He winks at me. "I'll be late, though."

"Why?"

"Because I want to walk you to your hut."

"You don't need to."

"I know I don't need to, Em. I *want* to."

"I know you do." I press my lips to his stubbled cheek. "But I don't want you to be late. People are going to want their Scotty specials."

"I do make a mean pineapple and passion fruit smoothie," he says. "You should come by for one later."

"I will," I promise. "And I'll bring your shirt back."

"Keep it." He touches my cheek, making sparks shoot through me. "I kind of like the thought of you having it." He brushes his lips over mine and then hops over the bar. A second later, he tosses me a bottle of water. "Drink it all. Then have another when you get back to your hut, okay?"

I nod and smile, pulling the cap off the water and taking a long, soothing drink.

I walk back to my hut on a cloud.

I slide my keycard through the door, and—

I gasp.

Lucifer Black.

Sitting on my bed, staring at one of the canvases I've been working on.

He doesn't look up.

He doesn't need to.

"Not your best work, Emily."

I don't reply.

"Then again, I was always your muse."

Still, I say nothing.

"You didn't truly think you could escape from me, did you?"

He rises, then, and turns toward me, his blue eyes on fire.

"Pack your things. We're going home. Now."

"No," I say.

He shakes his head. "Whose shirt is that?"

"No one's."

"You're not that good a liar, Emily."

"How did you get in here?"

He scoffs. "Really? You think I'm a vampire or something? That I need an invitation? We both knew I'd find you."

"But security—"

"I know my way around the best security in the world. How do you think I've remained in business so long? Now pack up."

"No." This time I plant my hands on my hips, determined. I just spent the most exciting night of my life, and I'm not ready for my time here to end.

I summon every ounce of strength I possess, every ounce of courage, every ounce of sheer guts.

Lucifer's power over me ends today.

"This isn't up for negotiation, Emily."

"I'm not going."

His fist comes toward me in slow motion. Nothing I haven't seen before, but this time—this time—I'm ready.

I know this man's moves. He doesn't strike me often, only when he feels I've disobeyed him.

Fleeing here is the ultimate disobedience in Lucifer's eyes.

The best block?

The best block is to not be there. Another lesson from Buck.

I duck, and then I run out the door.

## 16

## SCOTTY

"Scotty!" Nemo sidles up to the bar. "Someone didn't make it home last night."

"Someone thinks that's none of your business."

"Someone also forgot to put on a shirt this morning."

I don't respond. Normally I'd laugh off his comment, but I don't. I'm not irked. Not in the slightest. I just feel...

I should have walked Em back to her hut. To hell with my shift. She's more important.

"Last anyone saw, you grabbed two beers and disappeared."

"Still not your business."

"Well, if you're not interested in telling me about your evening, I'll tell you about mine."

"Lauren?" I ask.

"You betcha. And get this—she hates monogamy!"

"I know. She says anthropology doesn't support it."

"Yeah, whatever. I dig her outlook, man."

I laugh. Nemo always becomes a seventies reject after he gets laid. Never fails. "Glad you had fun."

"The whole thing became kind of an orgy after you left," Nemo says. "It rocked."

I nod. "Glad you had fun."

"You a broken record or something?"

"Huh?"

"You said that twice. 'Glad you had fun.'"

"Did I?"

"I figured once I said the word orgy your interest would be piqued."

Funny. Normally it would be. But not today. All I can think about is watching Emily walk away from me with only my island print shirt covering her. I can't wait to peel it off her later.

Damn.

I should have walked her back.

"What can I get you this morning, Nemo?"

"Still no comment on the orgy?"

"Not today. You want a smoothie? Juice? Water? Coconut water?"

"Give me a strawberry banana smoothie with a shot of wheatgrass."

I stare toward the path that leads to the colonists' huts. Something feels off to me. I can't put it into words, but the back of my neck feels like shards of ice are prickling it.

"Dude," Nemo says. "My smoothie."

I hop over the counter. "Do me a favor. Cover for me."

"I'm no bartender."

"Fake it."

"Scotty, what the fuck?"

"Sorry. There's something I need to do. Now."

"But—"

"For God's sake, Nemo, you know how to work a blender. All the recipes are under the counter. I'll be right back."

I'm still barefoot, wishing I had my Air Jordans, but I run. I don't know why, but I know I need to run.

I need to run fast.

I race through the common area and toward the colonists' huts—toward Emily's hut.

That's when I see her.

Still wearing my island print shirt.

My heart nearly jumps out of my chest as I swallow a gulp of air.

A blond man is holding her, a knife to her neck.

Security guards and island police officers have guns trained on him.

*God, please don't shoot. Please don't shoot. If they shoot him, they might get her.*

I can't bear the thought.

"Emily!" I shout.

She meets my gaze, pure fear in her brown eyes. She shakes her head slightly at me.

"Put the knife down," one of the officers says. "Put it down and we'll talk. You don't come out of this alive if you don't."

"Fuck off!" the blond man says.

My gut is twisting into knots. Acid claws up my throat.

"Emily!" I yell again, my voice hoarse.

The man whispers something to her. She shakes her head vehemently.

"Let her go!" I yell. "Take me instead!"

A security guard grabs me. "You've got to get out of here, Scotty. This isn't a game."

"Do I look like I think it's a game?" I wrench myself free from the guard, who I recognize as Jimmy Cox. We play poker sometimes.

"This guy's off his rocker," Jimmy says. "Get out of here before you get yourself in trouble."

"I don't care," I say. "I can't let him hurt her."

"We won't let him hurt her," Jimmy says. "You've got trust us. He's way outnumbered."

"I'm not worried about his life. Kill the SOB for all I care. I'm worried about *hers*."

"Scotty, for God's sake, let us do our job. If I'm here worrying about you, I'm not focused on her."

That's all I need to hear.

I step back, my heart in my throat being eaten alive by the bile that's coating it.

God, Em.

I knew she was hiding something. I just had no idea

it was a psycho boyfriend.

He looks vaguely familiar to me. He's tall, muscular, with light blond hair. Where have I seen him before?

My mind blanks.

Only Em. Her safety. That silver blade is right against the creaminess of her neck. The neck I spent last night kissing...

My God...

I can't lose her.

I can't lose Emily.

I rake my fingers through my hair, pace around behind the action. I could run forward, demand to help.

But Jimmy's right. I'm just another target the guards have to worry about.

I pace and pace and pace, until finally I turn back toward Emily and get as close as I can.

She meets my gaze.

And she mouths three words.

*I love you.*

God. I love you.

"I love you too," I mouth back.

I don't even have to think twice. The words tumble out on their own, as if they've always been inside me and always will be.

Is it forever love?

Does it even matter?

It's love, and if, God forbid, Em doesn't get out of this alive, I want her to know I love her.

In fact, I want to shout from the rooftops, but I don't want to startle the psycho.

My stomach churns. I haven't eaten anything. Just drank a quart of water when I got to the bar to begin my shift.

And now...

Now my stomach threatens to turn inside out on itself.

But Emily needs me.

She needs me to be strong for her.

Fuck! I feel so useless! So ridiculous standing here in nothing but board shorts, not allowed to cross the arbitrary line the guards have set up.

"Let her go," an officer with a bullhorn shouts. "You hurt her, you go down."

"If I die, we both die!" Psycho shouts back.

I curl my hands into fists. Not on my watch. I can't just stand here and do nothing.

I run.

I run full force through the makeshift boundary.

I run toward the woman I love.

I'm almost there when—

A shot. A fucking bullet.

## 17

## EMILY

Lucifer drops the knife and falls to the ground.
In a flash I'm running.

Running toward Scotty. "Scotty!"

I land in his arms and my mouth finds his.

We kiss hard. Deep. A kiss of life.

Time suspends itself.

We're in a warp. Everything around us ceases to exist.

We kiss.

We kiss.

We kiss.

"Scotty."

"Scotty."

"Scotty!"

He pulls away from me.

"Scotty." From one of the guards. "We need to talk to the lady."

Scotty's lips are swollen and pink from our kiss. Our feral kiss that I wish were still going on.

"Come with me." I tug on his hand.

He simply nods.

A minute later, we're sitting with Roy Wolfe himself and—

"Buck!" I launch myself at my brother.

"God, sis. Thank God." He kisses the top of my head.

"When did you get here?"

"When Lucifer did. I've been watching him since you left. Somehow I lost him for a span of fifteen minutes, and the next thing I knew, he was on a plane. Once he was on his way, so was I."

"Were you the sniper?" Scotty asks.

"Who the hell are you? And why were you kissing my sister?"

"Sorry," I say. "Buck, this is Scotty. Scotty, my brother."

Buck holds out his hand.

Scotty takes it. "Thanks, man. You saved the day."

"All in a day's work."

"Buck's an ex-Navy SEAL," I say.

"Emily, Scotty," Roy Wolfe says, "I'm so sorry for all of this. We'll be taking a good long look at our security systems."

"It's not your system," Buck says. "It's top-notch. I should know, since I advised you on it. Lucifer Black has gotten through top-notch security before. I'm just sorry I couldn't stop him from getting here. I'm sorry, Emily. I thought you'd be safe here."

I shake my head. "I know you did. This isn't your fault. I'm not safe anywhere as long as Lucifer is free."

"He's won't be free now," Buck says. "These are charges that will finally stick. We've got a ton of witnesses."

Roy's phone buzzes. "Excuse me." He puts it to his ear. "Yes?"

Pause.

"Thank you. I'll let everyone know."

"Mr. Ashton's injury is not life-threatening. He'll be transferred on a medical yacht to Hawaii where he'll be hospitalized and under constant guard. I assume you'll be filing charges, Ms. Moreno."

I nod, shivering. "Yes. Of course."

"We'll be doing a full investigation on how he got onto the island," Roy says.

"I can tell you right now how he got here," Buck says. "Money. He paid off a few of your people."

"Find them," Roy says, "and take care of them."

"Consider it done."

"People need to feel safe here," Roy says. "This can't ever happen again."

"Mr. Wolfe?" I say.

"Roy, please."

"Roy." I clear my throat. "He was determined to get to me. I should never have come here. I'm sorry."

"Don't be. Buck talked to me beforehand about your situation. I'm sorry we failed to protect you."

"You did protect me," I say. "All he had was a knife. His weapon of choice is a handgun, which clearly he couldn't bring here."

"I'm still very sorry, Ms. Moreno."

I smile. "Emily, please."

"Emily. What can Charlie and I do to make this up to you?"

"Nothing. You don't owe me anything."

"I've taken a look at your work. You're a very talented artist, especially with color mixing. Would you be interested in teaching here at the colony?"

My jaw drops. "You mean, live here?"

"Yes. You'll live over in the staff huts."

"With Scotty?"

Roy chuckles. "Well, not with Scotty. But in the same area."

I want to pounce on this offer, but—

"I'm not sure."

"Em," Buck says, "this is a great offer. You'll be able to paint to your heart's content. Work on your craft while you help others with theirs."

"It is a dream come true," I say.

I'll be free. Finally free from Lucifer's invisible bonds.

But Scotty...

I'm pretty sure he mouthed the words "I love you

too" when I mouthed "I love you," but we were in a life-or-death situation.

I don't want him to feel trapped.

And he was here first.

"May I think about it?"

"Of course." Roy rises. "I'll leave Jimmy here to get your official statement. Come talk to me when you decide."

ONE OFFICIAL STATEMENT LATER, Scotty and I are walking hand in hand back to my hut. I'm shivering.

"I can't stay here any longer. All I see in here is him, sitting on my bed, as if he owns the place."

"Baby, why didn't you tell me?"

"Because you would have run away screaming."

"No. I wouldn't have. I already knew you had some kind of baggage. That you were running away. If you'd come to my place last night instead of here—"

"He'd have found me anyway, and he wouldn't have thought twice of hurting you to get to me. Nothing stops him."

"Except your brother's bullet."

"Lucifer—"

"I knew I recognized him from somewhere," Scotty says. "He's Lucifer Ashton. From the Ashtons of LA. Is it true? The rumors?"

"That he's an underground drug kingpin? Yeah, they're all true."

"Emily"—he caresses my cheek—"my God. How did you..."

"He lavished me with gifts. With a life a starving artist could only dream about. I was seduced by the lifestyle, and gradually, I..." I shake my head. How can I admit what happened? What I *allowed* to happen?

"Damn, Em. Thank God you're okay."

"He trapped me. Wouldn't let me go anywhere without him, until the day I escaped. Buck sent me here. Then..."

"It's my fault." Scotty rubs his forehead, messes with his hair. "I should have walked you back this morning. None of this would have happened."

"Oh, Scotty." I entwine my fingers through his. "This isn't your fault at all. It's my fault. I stopped watching my back. I shouldn't have, but I did. *Carpe diem*, as you say."

"I wouldn't have said it if I thought it could get you killed."

"No. Don't go there," I say. "Last night with you was the most amazing night of my life. I'll never regret it."

He smiles. "Then stay here, Em. On the island. With me. And I promise we'll have many more nights even better than last night."

"You mean it? You want me to stay here? I may need some...counseling. To get over what I've been through and all."

"There just happens to be a top-notch retreat center

on the other side of the cliff with the best therapists in the world."

"You want me?" I ask. "Baggage and all?"

Scotty smiles, kisses my lips. "Baby, I want it all. And you've made me think about a lot of things."

"Like what?"

"Like maybe going back to school. I could take online courses and still work here. Maybe become a counselor myself."

"You did major in psychology. That's a wonderful idea." I brush his hair off his forehead and return his smile. "I thought of a name for your cocktail."

"You mean *our* cocktail"—he trails a finger over my lower lip—"my love?"

"Yeah. We'll call it the Island Escape."

Enjoy more Wolfes with the Wolfes of Manhattan and the Gems of Wolfe Island!

## ISLAND ESCAPE

1 shot gold rum

1 shot crème de banana

1 shot crème de noyaux

3 shots orange juice

3 shots pineapple juice

Shake with ice and strain into martini glasses rimmed with sugar.

## A NOTE FROM HELEN

Dear Reader,

Thank you for reading *Escape*. If you want to find out about my current backlist and future releases, please visit my website, like my Facebook page, and join my mailing list. If you're a fan, please join my street team to help spread the word about my books. I regularly do awesome giveaways for my street team members.

If you enjoyed the story, please take the time to leave a review on Goodreads and Amazon. I welcome all feedback.

I wish you all the best!

Helen

http://www.helenhardt.com/signup

## ACKNOWLEDGMENTS

Thank you so much to the following individuals who helped make *Escape* shine: Karen Aguilera, Linda Pantlin Dunn, Serena Drummond, Christie Hartman, Kim Killion, and Angela Tyler.

## ABOUT THE AUTHOR

#1 *New York Times*, #1 *USA Today*, and #1 *Wall Street Journal* bestselling author Helen Hardt's passion for the written word began with the books her mother read to her at bedtime. She wrote her first story at age six and hasn't stopped since. In addition to being an award-winning author of romantic fiction, she's a mother, an attorney, a black belt in Taekwondo, a grammar geek, an appreciator of fine red wine, and a lover of Ben and Jerry's ice cream. She writes from her home in Colorado, where she lives with her family. Helen loves to hear from readers.

Please sign up for her newsletter here:
http://www.helenhardt.com/signup
Visit her here:
http://www.helenhardt.com

Made in United States
North Haven, CT
09 February 2022